Sounds in the Cellar

by Frances Ann Ladd

Illustrated by Duendes del Sur

D0888276

SCHOLASTIC INC.

New York   Toronto   London   Auckland   Sydney
Mexico City   New Delhi   Hong Kong   Buenos Aires

Scritch! Scratch!
"Jeepers!
What was that
strange sound?"
said Shaggy.
"It came from the cellar."
Shaggy opened
the cellar door.
Creak! went the hinge.

"Scooby, are you
in the cellar?"
Shaggy yelled.
There was no answer.
Shaggy got a flashlight.
Then he went
down the stairs.

Shaggy looked around the cellar. "Gee, this place gives me the creeps!" he said.

Scritch! Scratch!
"There is the strange
sound again!
I heard it twice!"
Shaggy said.
"It sounds like danger!"

EEE-EEE-EEE
went a squeaky voice.
"I'm scared!"
said Shaggy.
"I wish I knew
where Scooby was.
But there is
no trace of him!"

Then Shaggy saw
a huge shadow
on the cement wall.
"Maybe it's
a gigantic monster!"
Shaggy said.
"Maybe it's
a giant ghost!"

Just then
Scooby turned on
the cellar light.
Shaggy saw what made
the strange sound.
He saw what made
the huge shadow.

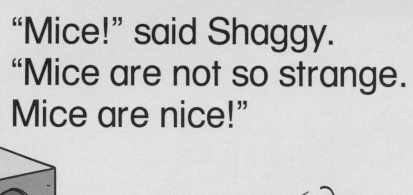

"Mice!" said Shaggy.
"Mice are not so strange.
Mice are nice!"